For Frances

Over many long miles
and many short years

love,

js

Acknowledgments:
To my friends, Mae Andersen Krieger, who runs with the wind, Kathleen Andersen, who chases after Mae and the wind, and Jonathan Krieger, who waits patiently;
to the Mackinsons, Ayrshires, and porcupines of Cayuga Ridge; to Nina Gruener, Amy Novesky, and Melissa Greenberg at Cameron Kids—
who build strong, healthy books nine different ways; and to Abigail Samoun and her Red Fox for her thoughtfulness and good counsel – my thanks! js

Library of Congress Cataloging-in-Publication Data available.

ISBN: 978-1-944903-73-2

Printed in China

10 9 8 7 6 5 4 3 2 1

Cameron Kids is an imprint of Cameron + Company

Cameron + Company
Petaluma, CA 94952
www.cameronbooks.com

OAK LEAF

John Sandford

cameron kids

Autumn arrived quietly
so no one would notice.
But the trees knew.

Oak Leaf changed from green to yellow, orange, and red.

It waved goodbye to its friends and left on a fall breeze.

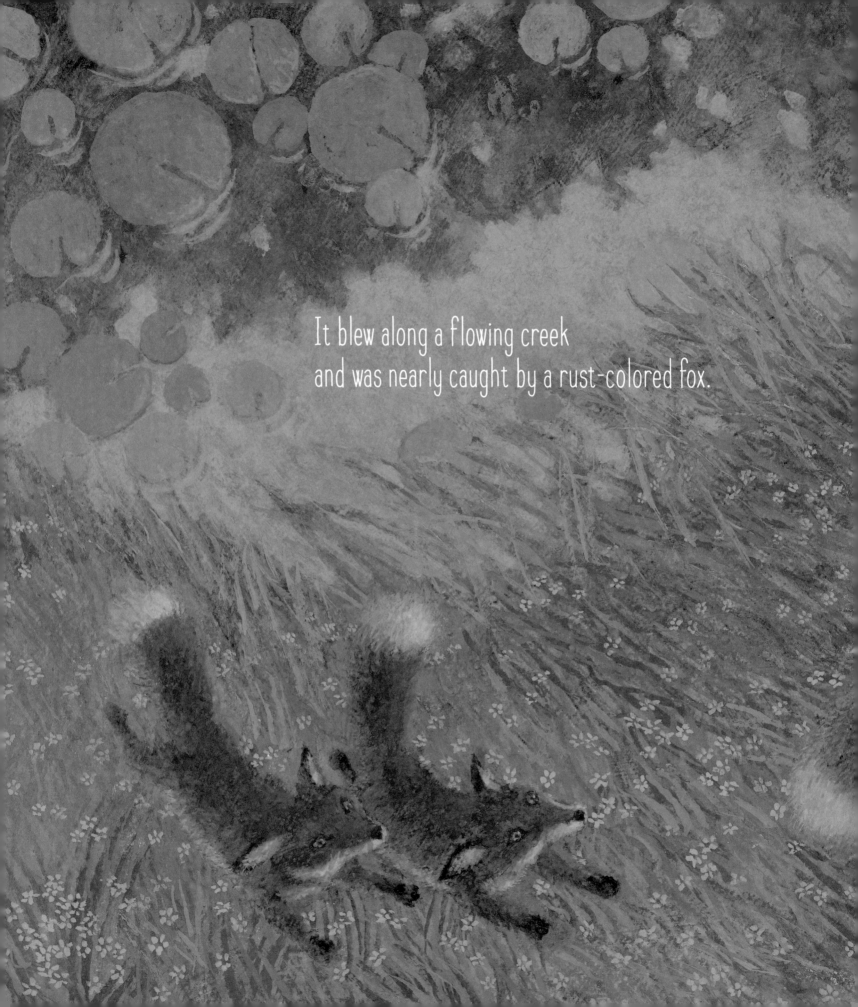

It blew along a flowing creek
and was nearly caught by a rust-colored fox.

Only to fly aloft and away in the

rrrrrush

of a freight train.

Over Mackinson's farm,
over the barn and silos,
over the cows in the pasture.

Where it rested a moment, on the nose of a calf, until —

Shwooosh – caught in a gust, it rushed

through the fingers of bare branches,

past a flock of maple leaves.

Over the freezing lake waters,
and then up into the sky once more.

Up through the mist,
away from earth, up.

Up toward the clouds.

Up to the edge of the sky
where the world tilted.

There Oak Leaf paused,
then dropped—
down through clouds,
down through a V of geese.

Down to a colorful city below.

To the left of a plaza.

To the right of a statue.

Spinning, spiraling, tumbling.

Circling, fluttering, falling.

Then caught.

Carefully pressed between
the leaves of a book.

And kept.

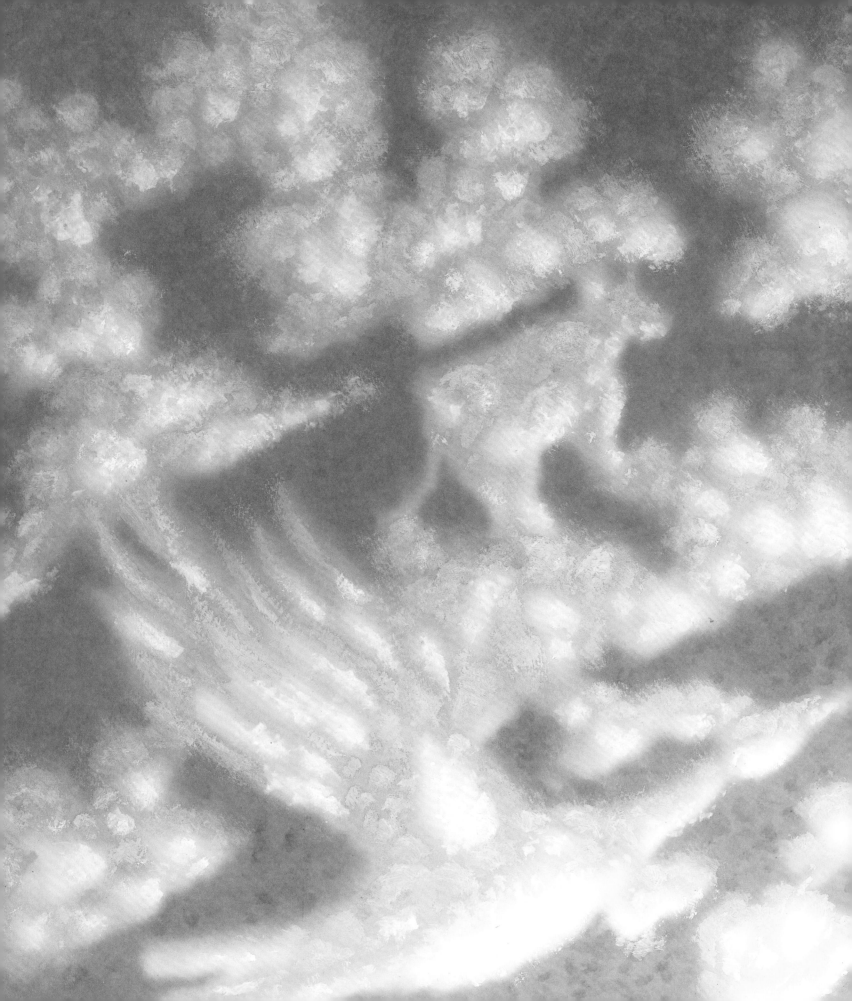